CHINESE WOMEN

PJ42014

JAN LOWE SHINEBOURNE

CHINESE WOMEN
A NOVEL

PEEPAL TREE

First published in Great Britain in 2010
Peepal Tree Press Ltd
17 King's Avenue
Leeds LS6 1QS
England

ISBN13: 9781845231514

The characters and events in this novel are fictitious.
Any resemblance to any persons, living or dead, is
purely coincidental.

Supported by
ARTS COUNCIL
ENGLAND

And I am come down to deliver them out of the hand of the Egyptians, and to bring them up out of that land unto a good and spacious land, unto a land flowing with milk and honey, unto the place of the Canaanites, and the Hittites, and the Amorites, and the Perizzites, and the Hivites, and Jebusites.

Exodus 3: 8

1

When I met Alice Wong in 1961, I was only fourteen. I met Anne Carrera in 1961 too. Both of them left me with a love of Chinese women that lasted almost fifty years and is strong enough to last another fifty. That is why I decided to look for Alice again in 2006 and marry her, though almost forty years had passed with no contact between us.

But I failed to marry Alice and now I realise that 1961, not 2006, was the year that really sealed my fate. 1961 determined that a dozen years later I would join the exodus fleeing Guyana for Canada, where I became wealthy and successful, and Chinese women, including Anne Carrera and Alice Wong, really had nothing to do with it, though I've believed that Alice Wong, more than anyone or anything, made my life better. I even thought she saved my life.

★   ★   ★   ★

My name is Albert Aziz. I was born in British Guiana in 1947.

In 1957, I fell a hundred feet and broke all the major joints in my body when I climbed to the top of a genip tree to reach a bunch of the delicious purple fruit. I held on with my left hand and stretched my right as far as I could. I knew I couldn't reach but forced myself to stretch from head to toe, willing myself to succeed, refusing to think about the danger of falling, confident my will would overcome my physical limitations and make me succeed. I did not know my limits. I was a little god, a spoilt boy in a family of mainly girls, treated like a prince by my doting mother, who called me *Sonny* to show her pride in having a son, a pride she did not feel in having daughters. When I began to fall, I knew I was falling from my throne to something I deserved for my arrogance and conceit, and I allowed myself to fall willingly. I opened my arms and legs like wings to make me fly. Though so young, I was willing to embrace death because I thought it would free my sisters from the oppression my birth had brought them; they would be well rid of me. When I hit the ground, I felt no pain, or if I did, I told myself I didn't. I blanked my feelings. I did not allow myself to feel any pain. I never have.

After my fall, my mother shrieked hysterically. It made me hate her even more than I already did, for behaving like lower-class Indian women at funerals, shrieking and weeping hysterically for show. Initially, she did not leave my side in the hospital, but after a month, she and my father moved far away, to Berbice, so that I only saw them once a month for the next three years. They abandoned me in the Georgetown Hospital. If my mother had loved me, she would never have let my father take that job in Berbice. It could have waited until I was better. When I begged them not to go to Berbice, they laughed and said Berbice was "the land of milk and honey", and they had to go.

Before Berbice, we used to live at Enmore Estate on the East Coast, Demerara, where we were dirt poor. The job in Berbice gave him all the money and status in the world, or so it seemed to them. At Enmore, my father worked in junior management for Bookers Sugar Estates. He'd done that since he was thirty. At fifty, to be offered a job in Berbice in senior management, to become an overseer among the expatriate white overseers, was to reach the very top. It elevated him beyond the dreams of most Indian men in the colony. In 1957, sugar estate Indians in Guiana still lived in degrading poverty, ignorance and backwardness. Before Berbice, no one in our family ever finished primary school. In Berbice, my sisters and I went to high school. This helped me get into university in Toronto and study engineering. My father becoming an overseer in British Guiana in 1957 was equivalent to me becoming a millionaire in 2000, when I sold my first nuclear centrifuge design in the Middle East for a million US dollars.

When they made that decision, I knew they did not love me as much as they loved money, if they could abandon me at death's door because he wanted more money.

In the nineteenth century, my ancestors were taken from India to British Guiana in ships, like the African slaves they were sent to replace on the sugar estates. Indians, both Hindus and Muslims, were the new slaves, but the Hindus did not want to be identified with us, the Muslims, so they called us *Fulamen*, after the African Muslim Fulani tribe who were among the original slaves in the Caribbean. I grew up at Enmore used to being called *Fulaman*. It was always an insult, a way of telling me not to get too big for my boots, and remember I was just a slave.

The fact that after several generations my father was still working on a sugar estate was a sign we had failed to progress from slavery. The Africans had long escaped the sugar plantation and some joined the middle class by becoming Christian and educated, a path Indian Muslims did not take, preferring to make money by buying land, renting property and loaning money – a long, painstaking path to betterment. My father's promotion to overseer catapulted us, overnight, into the white middle-class to live in luxury and privilege among the white expatriate overseers.

I may have been only ten and paralysed in my hospital

bed while the rest of my family moved up in the world, but in my mind, I was moving up with them, too. I had no intention of being left back, or left out.

British Guiana was a colony ruled by racism and snobbery. The British ruled at the top, so their white skin became a status symbol. They enslaved the brown Indian and Black African. The lighter your skin colour, the higher your status, the darker, the lower. The Portuguese also came to the country to work as labourers on the sugar estates, but because their skin was white, they became second in power to the British. The coloureds and mixed race people took education and worked in the civil service and middle-class professions, so they were third in status. Thus, the black or brown skin of the African and Indian, the races at the bottom, became a symbol of failure and held you back.

To grow up in British Guiana was to learn all the codes of racial snobbery and prejudice that surrounded our differences of appearance and culture. You learned these codes of prejudice daily from the cradle – from gossip you heard in your family, your neighbourhood, the streets and school. We were all like spiders, constantly weaving a web of racial intrigue around each other, even in the hospital among the sick and dying. There was no escaping it. This was the society the British created for us to live in, a racist society.

I entered the hospital a brown-skinned Indian boy with

a hysterical Indian mother shrieking as if ready to fling herself on my funeral pyre. Seeing this low-class Indian behaviour, or the behaviour of *Coolies* as they called the Indians, the African nurses treated us with unconcealed contempt. From my first day there, I knew I was not going to be looked after and while the fall had not killed me, the nurses well might do that, simply through neglect. They gave me the feeling that just for being a *Coolie* I deserved to die.

In our country, Africans and Indians did not bother to conceal their hatred for each other. Both were dragged in chains to the country to labour like brute animals, but instead of uniting them to fight the white man who oppressed and divided them, they guarded their separate lives, jealously resenting and wishing the worst on each other.

At the age of ten, there I lay in the hospital, in need of the healing care of my countrymen, knowing they were not capable of giving it, neither by instinct, nor by training, for the standards of the hospital were known to be very low. People joked that if you went in there, you would not come out alive. Infection was so rife, it was the biggest killer in the hospital. My mother knew that, yet she abandoned me there. The parents of the coloured children came in every day to keep an eye on them, to ensure they were being treated well, and let the nurses and doctors know they were expecting them to be looked after. It was part of being middle class to expect a high standard of service. My parents had never learned to be middle class like the coloureds, so they abandoned me in hospital to the care of the Blacks who hated us. To my mother and father, self-improvement was about making money and being able to buy things, not improving your behaviour or values. So, how was I ever going to learn to know better?

There was never anything but superstition, ignorance and fear surrounding my Muslim identity in British Guiana. On Fridays in Enmore, when we went to the mosque for prayers, the Blacks and Hindus would shout at us, "Fula people! Fula *coolie!*"

I asked my parents why they were calling us these names. They explained about the Fulani Muslim slaves from Africa, but reassured me that being a Muslim did not make me like a Black slave. I was Indian, my ancestors came from Kashmir in India. They said it was better to be an Indian than an African because Indians had not become degraded like them. They said that so degraded was the African, that as soon as he collected his pay, he went straight to the dancehall where the many mothers of his many illegitimate children waited with outstretched hands to collect their share. What was left, he spent at the whorehouse and rumshop, giving it all away, not saving a penny. The Indian was the opposite. When he collected his pay, he went straight to the post office where he deposited half of it in a savings account; the rest he spent carefully on the necessities of life – on maintaining his house, and on food and clothing for his family. For the

Indian, money was precious, not to be wasted. If the Indian found a cent in the street or in his pocket, he put it in his savings account. They came from India to British Guiana with the values of thrift and ambition, and kept these values for generations.

My parents told me that, as for the Hindus, calling us *Fulamen* just showed their cowardice. They wanted to ensure they were not at the bottom of the pile in Guiana, that they were not treated like slaves, so they put us, their fellow Indians, in that position instead. It was their way of telling people to pick on us instead of them. Though they were Indian like us, Hindus would always betray us. So, I learned early not to trust Blacks and Hindus, the two groups that ended up ruling Guiana and chasing us out of the country.

For three years, I lay in my hospital bed, watching the Black nurses come and go. I felt better knowing I was not a slave like them, and distanced myself completely from them, especially when they touched me. When a black nurse touched me, I would compare the colour of my skin with theirs, and rejoice that my skin was not black as tar but brown as a sapodilla – though I knew it was the reason they might kill me.

My luck turned when an English doctor, Dr. Webster, began to take a special interest in me, and made it his mission to heal my body, using all the latest techniques of fracture repair from England. He applied his best knowledge to getting me better, and trained the nurses to take care of me. Painstakingly, slowly, Dr. Webster reset my joints and ligaments until they grew back and I became whole and began to leave my bed and take short walks around the hospital. He said my recovery was like a miracle. I asked him to explain a miracle. He said it was when someone got better not because of medical help but because of their determination, and strength of mind, and I was his little miracle. He also said it was like magic and he called me a magician. He wrote papers about me and published them in England. He showed me the medical journals they appeared in. There was my name, Albert Aziz, with my photographs. He called me his "star" and treated me like his son. He liked to bring me presents – toys and books from England he asked his mother in London to send. He even baked cakes for me, and brought books to read to me. He liked Greek mythology and told me it was important to know the Greek myths. He said they were full of heroes and if I knew the myths, they would turn me into a hero. He gave me a book, *A Children's Encyclopaedia of Greek Mythology*. I kept it for a long time but I never read it. When I left for Canada in 1974, I threw it away.

Sometimes I wonder if Dr. Webster was homosexual. He was not married, he did not have a girlfriend. Everyone knows Englishmen are all homosexuals. My father said so, and he should know; he worked with them all his life.

Dr. Webster gave me a quiz game called *Magic Robot*. He said the robot was a magician like me. The robot held a long wand. He fitted into a notch in the middle of a circle of questions. You rotated the robot until his wand pointed to a question, then you put him on the mirror in the middle of a circle of answers. He spun round on the mirror and came to rest with his wand pointing at the correct answer. I never tired of playing with the magic robot. Seeing how I loved it, Dr. Webster arranged for me to have private lessons in Maths and English twice a week and paid for it himself.

In 1960, Dr. Webster reluctantly discharged me from Georgetown Hospital to go to Berbice and live with my family again. He told me he was not happy to send me so far away. When he told me this, it sounded so personal, like a lover, but by then, I was used to his intimate and loving way of talking to me. I put it down to him being an Englishman and like all of them, having a tendency to prefer little boys to women.

★   ★   ★   ★

In 1960, when I first saw the overseer's compound in Berbice where my family now lived, and the magnificent house the estate gave us, I felt we were now rich and free at last. For two years, I had been in plastercast and splints, walking and moving for less than a year. It had all made me very depressed, but when I saw my luxurious new home, it lifted my spirits because I felt I would never be poor again.

I remember the car turning into the overseers' compound, and feeling overwhelmed by the sight of the rows of large, beautiful houses surrounded by manicured lawns and flower beds. When my sisters visited me in hospital, they used to tell me about the fantastic luxury in which they now lived, in a house maintained by servants who cooked their meals, washed and ironed their clothes, cleaned the house, cut the grass, watered the plants and ran their smallest errands. There was a swimming pool and a social club they were allowed to share with the white overseers. They swam in the swimming pool with white people, and at the social club they ate and drank the same English food as the white people – mashed potato, sandwiches with lettuce and tomato, potato chips and beef steaks. They could even go to their dances and dance beside them. It was like a fairy tale to live as equals of the white overseers. My sisters hopped with excitement when they described the life they were living in Berbice.

Our house was so luxurious; there were screens on the windows to keep out flies and mosquitoes – a luxury ordinary Guyanese could never afford, accepting their vulnerability to flying pests and the diseases they spread. Only white expatriates used those screens, so they were a status symbol that set us apart as a privileged elite. When I saw the screens on our house, I felt like a little maharajah approaching his palace. I looked forward to living like a little white man.

In our house, there were five bedrooms for eight of us.

My four sisters and my brother, Rupert, shared four bedrooms. Dr. Webster suggested I should have a bedroom of my own, to help my recuperation, but this idea created dissent in my family. Everyone except my mother objected to me getting such a major privilege. She tried to persuade them to let me have my own room, the en suite bedroom. My father objected the most. He had always hated my mother treating me like a little prince and was not prepared to put up with it again. He had enjoyed not having me around, and resented my return. He always complained he had too many mouths to feed. While I was in hospital, there was one mouth less to feed, Now I was back, I was just another mouth to eat into his money. I was not welcome.

When lunch was served, we sat around a large, polished mahogany dining table like white people, ate with knives and forks, and placed paper napkins in our laps, something I had never seen my family do. At Enmore, we used to sit on the floor and eat with our hands. I could see they were uncomfortable with the eating implements, but they were determined to persist, though they were eating chicken curry and roti, a meal we always ate with our hands. My father sat at the head of the table; he looked extremely nervous and uncomfortable. I noticed he had acquired a severe facial tic, and sweated so profusely, his shirt was always completely soaked. As we ate, servants fussed over us, refilling our glasses of Coca Cola, sweeping the floor under the table, wiping it clean as soon as anything was dropped. I noticed that my siblings had developed haughty expressions, and treated the servants dismissively, barking orders at them, and giving them cutting, contemptuous looks.

When my mother realised she could not persuade my siblings to let me to have my own room, she told my father he should force them to do it. When darkness fell and they began to go to bed, she took me to the bedroom she shared with my father and installed me in their bed. When my father entered and saw me lying there like a little prince, he went berserk. He opened a cupboard, pulled out a great length of electrical cord and began to wield it like a whip, swishing and curling it through the air like a lasso. He bellowed threats to my siblings, and I could hear them all screaming in a chorus of hysteria. He ran to their rooms and began to whip them. Sometimes, he ran back into the bedroom, dragging one of my sisters by her hair along the floor, kicking and punching and whipping them. Tears and saliva dripped from them and formed a trail into the room. At one stage, he pointed to me and screamed, "You will get the same treatment, you wait!"

That night, he slept on the veranda while my sisters blubbered inhumanly in their sleep. The noises they made merged into the sounds of the night crickets and frogs outside. I thought I also heard a very unfamiliar human sound, far away – the sound of children laughing, but I thought I was dreaming.

$\star$ $\star$ $\star$ $\star$

I was not dreaming. As I woke in the morning, I heard the same sounds – the unmistakable sound of children laughing. It was coming from outside. I had dreaded having to get up in the morning and face my father, convinced he would carry out his threat to whip me with the electric cord, so it was with relief that I saw him get dressed and leave very early, ignoring me.

As soon as I could, I went to the window and looked outside. There, playing and laughing on the lawn of the house next door, were two, small, dark-haired white boys. They were so happy, and so free in their movements and laughter, I stayed at the window for a very long time watching them, even refusing to eat the breakfast my mother brought me. She saw me watching them and told me I was not to stand at the window staring at the white people. They would see me and complain to the manager about it, and my father would be angry if I upset the white people and he would beat me. I moved away from the window, but I went back to look as soon as I heard them again. I could not get enough of watching them. I saw their mother too – a tall woman with black hair and skin so pink I assumed she was white. She came downstairs a few times to talk to them. I strained to hear what she was saying but I couldn't, though the sound of her voice was very clear, floating on the air like music. When she spoke to them, the boys looked at her and smiled. They all seemed to smile constantly, something unknown in my scowling, cold and distant family. She must have called them indoors to breakfast because they disappeared inside for a while and then came back out to play cricket. She even joined in with them, hitting the ball far and laughing when they chased it, dropping the bat and chasing it too, racing with them. She played like a child, throwing her head back when she laughed so you could see her long, white throat and her eyes became shut. I loved this scene; it made me feel drunk. I leaned on the window, my head drooped and I fell asleep until my mother found me and began to upbraid me for being "fast" – our word for being inquisitive. She told me my father would beat me for staring at the white people. Nevertheless, I became addicted to standing at the window and staring at that family, especially the mother. It seemed she would go to any lengths to entertain her sons and make them happy. I watched to see what next she would do, always delighted when she invented new games for them.

I saw her husband come and go. He looked like a typical English overseer. He always smoked a pipe. He was tall and muscular and walked about his property like a king, arms akimbo, inspecting the work of the servants. I found out from the servants their name was Carrera, and her name was Anne Carrera.

The more I observed Anne Carrera from my window, the more convinced I became she might be an approachable white woman, perhaps someone who might even exchange a formal greeting with me. Many times, I saw her speaking in a sociable way with one of her servants, smiling with them, and it convinced me she might be friendly enough to speak with me if I could get near enough. It became my mission to meet or have some kind of contact with her. I would fantasise about it, imagining myself walking downstairs, crossing the road, stepping onto her lawn and speaking to her. I imagined her smiling and laughing with me, throwing back her head while the breeze ruffled her smooth black hair and the sun exposed her white throat. In my fantasy, I rehearsed this scene over and over, willing it to happen.

My mother was paranoid about letting me out of her sight. She blamed herself for my fall from the genip tree. My father had blamed her for not keeping a closer eye on me. One of my sisters told me he gave her a beating for it. She realised I was eager to go outdoors for some physical freedom but was afraid to let me out. She knew I got vicarious pleasure from watching the Carrera boys and longed to play with them. I knew I would never be allowed because they were white, but because Anne Carrera seemed such a nice woman, I harboured a fantasy she just might permit it, if she knew of my plight. I had no grounds for expecting this could happen; only the excitement and pleasure it gave me to watch her led me to imagine it. This fantasy was prohibited, but the imprint she made on me, just through the sheer pleasure of watching her, seemed to give me the willpower and strength of a man, and the day I saw her present her sons with a small puppy, and I saw those boys go running off towards the horizon chasing it, I felt a precocious and fearless little man enough to make my way to the front door, avoiding being heard or seen by my mother or the servants. With my heart pounding, I descended the stairs, crossed the road and stepped into the forbidden Carrera garden. I was so afraid, I expected something terrible to happen – a bolt of lightning to strike me, or the armed security guard at the entrance of the overseers' quarters to shoot me. I peed myself, feeling the hot urine trickle down my bare legs, through the hairs I was beginning to grow. I saw Anne Carrera running towards me, laughing, her sons running beside her, the puppy chasing them. While one part of my brain told me not to run towards her, the other told me to do so, and I did. I was not used to running; it was difficult – a miracle I could run at all. My knees buckled and I crashed to the ground, banging my elbows, which had not set properly. I decided to let my body relax and lie there like a foetus, waiting for my heart to slow and my breathing to become calm. I looked up to the sky as if in surrender, waiting for some miracle resurrection to pick me up and float me away to heaven, to paradise, just as I had done when I fell from the tree. I wanted to be dead and gone from a world where I was bound to get a beating from my father for stepping on the white man's property and daring to make contact with his wife and children.

I heard Anne Carrera's laughter as she stood over me, her skirt wrapped around her thighs in the breeze. One of her sons came and stood near her and wrapped himself round her thigh. She called him "Brian". Her other son she called "Michael". In the sunlight, their shadows fell across me and I felt as if they had touched me. My eyes stung with tears. I lifted a hand, hoping she would take it, and help me to my feet. Instead, I heard the hysterical shrieks of my mother, and felt her roughly pull me to my feet. She had brought the big, strong, black servant with her, Mavis. They grabbed an arm each and dragged me roughly across the lawn and the road. When we got to the stairs, my mother gave me a violent push and ordered me, "Go upstairs!" As I dragged myself up on my backside, I saw Mrs. Carrera trying to talk to my mother while my mother ignored her. There was so much feeling in Anne Carrera's eyes. I was so close to her, I wanted to wrap myself round her like Brian, but I just waved to her and she waved back. My mother saw this and a look of horror and shock passed across her face to see me being so familiar with a white woman.

Mavis helped me to the kitchen and sat me down at the table where I stayed for the rest of the day, my mother forbidding me to stand at the window and stare at the Carreras ever again.

Mournfully and wearily, my mother recited the usual mantra of rules pertaining to how we should behave with our white neighbours. We should not look at or speak to them, not assume any familiarity with them or trespass on their property. She enumerated the punishments that would follow from breaking these rules, the worst being my father losing his job, losing the house, his salary and never being employed by Bookers again.

So my family, though now living in the place they called the land of milk and honey, were also living in continual fear and terror of being thrown out. The white man gave us everything, but he could also take it all away.

*   *   *   *

My mother loved to gossip. It was her main form of communication with my sisters and the servants. I realised I could find out all I needed to know about Anne Carrera by gossiping with her. I took to following her around the house, looking for opportunities to get her alone.

Once, she went downstairs to take the washing off the line when Anne Carrera was playing with her sons. I sat on a chair and watched them.

"Why you always watching them?" she snapped.

"I don't have anything else to do," I replied.

"White people don't like when we watch them."

"I not watching white people. I watching them boys playing."

"You saying them boys not white?"

"No."

"You better be careful. Is not for you to say who white and who ain't. You think you white?"

Mavis was listening, and she said, "Them chil'ren ain't white, them is Chinee children. De mother is a chinee. Jus' because she married a white man don't make she white. We don't have no Chinee overseer here so she ain't got no right to live here."

My mother declared, "Even he ain't white, he is a Putagee! But he does play like he more white than the white man. All dem Putagee people, if they get a chance, like to play white, but Putagee can never be white. Putagee got big foot. You ever see white people with big foot? No man, them two boys ain't white, they ain't suppose to live here. Only white people can live here. Them children is half Putagee an' half Chinee but they going to the white children school, playing with the white children as if they white. That Chinee woman bareface. She playin' white; she ain't white."

Boldly, I said, "How you know Mrs. Carrera is Chinee? She look white to me."

Mavis snorted. "Since when Chinee does look white? She is a real Chinee. What you talking about? You ever see real Chinee people?"

My mother's brain was being exercised by the complex work of figuring out Anne Carrera's ethnicity and status with the servant. She declared, "No Mavis, she look white. She ain't got the real Chinee look. She nose straight, she skin colour pink. Chinee skin white like chalk. No, she look like a white lady, she ain't look Chinee. She can pass for white, she tall like a white woman, she got big bubby and big batty. Chinee women short short, they got flat bubby and batty, round nose. They face flat like a tawa. Mrs. Carrera got straight

straight nose, narrow face, long jaw, but she is Chinee, she don't fool me. She fooling everybody she and she children white. She know how to play white lady, but she is Chinee. Watch them two children. You don't see they got flat batty and Chinee crossway eye? They hair straight straight straight and black and thick like Chinee hair."

To figure out whether or not Anne Carrera *was* Chinese never became a reason for me to stand at the windows of our house and spy on her the way my mother and her servants did, studying her behaviour to ascertain whether they should defer to her or not.

Anne Carrera's ethnicity was of no real interest to me. It thrilled me to watch her play with her sons and sent something like an electric charge through me that made me feel strong.

I often saw the Carreras come and go with tennis racquets. I dreamed of playing tennis with them. I dreamed that if I could, that a miracle would happen, and I would regain my full powers of mobility.

*   *   *   *

We were not the only Indian Muslim family permitted to live among the whites. There was another one, the Insanallys. My sisters went to the local primary school with the Insanally girls who came to visit them. There were two boys. The youngest, Winston, was my age. I was being educated at home privately, to prepare me for the entrance exams to Berbice High School. Winston was bright and helped me with my studies. When I was ready, I asked him to keep me company on my first walk round the estate. He was eager to show off how well he knew the estate and took me to the biggest house, the manager's. The entrance was guarded by armed security guards, but he knew a secret way to get in, by climbing up the "white lady" guava tree that grew against the fence and jumping into the garden. Guava trees are difficult to climb, and we were just standing there trying to work out how to do it when the manager's wife, Mrs. Smith, appeared on the other side. In her hand, she held a gun. She pointed it at us and ordered us off her property. Winston begged her not to shoot us and ran away, leaving me alone with her.

"Get off my property you stupid *coolie*!" she ordered. At that moment, I wished I had a gun to point at her, to shoot her and all the whites, to rid us of the fear and terror of white people that plagued my family. To kill all of them would solve our problems.

I found Winston cowering and trembling under a tree. He really believed Mrs. Smith was going to use the gun on us. Only the apartheid regime on the estate could have convinced a small Indian boy that the whites had a licence to kill him.

I told him, "She can't kill you; the judge will lock her up or hang her."

"Which judge?" he retorted.

"The judge in the court."

He cried, "Yes! Dr. Jagan court. He will lock her up. He don't like overseers, he say they must leave our country. He want to get rid of Bookers, hand it over to us, the coolie people, because he is a coolie. He want we coolie to run the estate and the country."

All the talk in the country then was about the politics of Cheddi Jagan, the Hindu revolutionary communist, our Fidel Castro. Winston was just regurgitating it, like gossip. I was surprised because I thought the Insanallys knew better than to support a Hindu.

Winston declared, "My father say Jagan is a communist and the white people going to lock he up! Jagan is just a coolie man. He can't do the white man anything."

I couldn't resist asking Winston what race his parents said Anne Carrera was. He said they thought she was Chinese because she is crossway. He pointed to his eyes to indicate her eyes were like slits across her face. I shook my head and disagreed, insisting she was white. I believed my mother and her servants when they said she was passing herself off as white. I understood she was doing it to protect herself. I wanted to help her, I wanted to protect her. Whether she was white or Chinese, it did not matter to me. All that mattered was the intense satisfaction I got from watching her play with her sons. I had fallen in love with her because I wanted for myself the love and kindness she gave to her sons.

Winston was used to roaming freely round the estate and he took me everywhere – to the tennis courts, the swimming pool, the senior club, all the places only whites were allowed. Because we were two small boys just nosing around, the local staff turned a blind eye when they saw us messing around with the snooker table or round the pool. Winston told me his family were not afraid of mixing with the white people and often exercised their right to have access to the facilities, though they knew the whites did not like mixing with them. It did not stop them going to the dances and picnics; they used the tennis courts and swimming pool too. He told me his older brother, Imran, had learned to swim and play tennis, and I should learn so we could compete and beat the white boys like Brian and Michael Carrera who were only now learning to play tennis. I was sure I would never ever be strong enough to swim or play tennis. My right elbow had not set well, nor my knees. My arms and legs would never be straight, my elbow and knee joints did not work smoothly, and never would. I could not rely on them to make me fully mobile. In 1960, I knew I would never ever be able to play sports. Playing tennis or swimming like the Carrera boys was out of the question. I accepted I would always be a cripple and a spectator, and so I began to follow Winston round the estate, spending my days with him growing into manhood, watching the white men play their sports – tennis, cricket, snooker, darts – studying and admiring their agility and skills, knowing I could never be like them. The worst fate of the Black slave or the East Indian coolie was to be a spectator of the white man's lifestyle, knowing it was unattainable, knowing that he was forever orphaned from the white man's high standard of living, his wealth, property, luxuries, and his women.

As my legs had gradually become strong enough to walk me round the estate and take me to the tennis courts and sports club, I wondered whether anyone might be watching me the way I watched the Carreras, and what they made of me – this dark brown Indian teenager with the disjointed arms and legs, who moved like a robot, a clockwork creature that was once broken and had to be pieced together again by a white doctor who set his springs and screws again, who wound me up with a key and let me out so I could wind my way around his world.

After my discharge, I'd been taken by my parents to Georgetown for monthly checks with Dr. Webster. As usual he always took more than a medical interest in me. He always nagged my parents about my education. He was convinced I was very bright, even gifted.

Dr. Webster told my father to take me on tours round the sugar estate. He told him I liked science and would find it interesting to learn how the factory worked, and so my father began to do it. Mrs. Smith had complained to our families that Winston and I were stealing guavas from her tree. For this, we both got a thrashing. I got to experience what it was like to be whipped with the electric cord while my sisters scattered and screamed. I am sure Anne Carrera could hear when we were being thrashed and I wondered what she thought about it, whether it made her sad or whether she might even shed a tear of pity and sorrow for us. During the beatings, my mother would beg my father to stop but he always ignored her. He did not care if anyone knew he was beating his children. Still, he began to take me round the estate on his motor cycle, thinking it would satisfy my curiosity and stop me roaming about with Winston and getting into trouble.

The overseers were the only ones who drove motorised vehicles around the estate – an assortment of jeeps and motor cycles, mainly British motorcycles, RSA Bantam 250 c.c two stroke engines, until the better Japanese makes came along. They also owned the latest small cars – Morris Minors, Prefects, Wolseleys, Mini Minors. My father always took what he was given – an RSA Bantam, and a green Mini Minor. These machines were a godsend to me, a cripple. I easily learned to drive and repair them; I had a natural talent for machines and engines and I came to be known as an engineering genius. With engines and wheels, I forgot that my body was permanently damaged. Cars and machines became an extension of me. The motorcycle and car my father owned gave me wings to fly round the estate and helped me grow out of my fixation with Anne Carrera.

★   ★   ★   ★

My father was a field overseer. It was his job to rise at four in the morning and, by five, meet the population of estate labourers at the high bridge where he delegated work to them – how much cane they were to cut, how much weed to clear from the canals, how many punts of cane to load. Then, when the workers dispersed to do these dirtiest of jobs, his job was to follow and supervise them. If they did not perform well, he had to prompt them or sometimes discipline them. He liked to show me how he did this. It was not very different from his approach to his family. He used threats and verbal and physical abuse to frighten them into obedience. The white overseer did not have to do this. His mere presence was enough to impose his authority and power. He had only to drive by on his motorcycle or in his Land Rover for the workers to increase the speed of their work or cut short their rest. They did not respect my father like this. He was just a short, balding, overweight East Indian man with a facial tic and bandy legs. Instead of addressing him respectfully as "Mr", they called him by his surname, Aziz, or called him names – *Fulaman* or *Bowfoot*. To win my respect, he took me to work with him to see how much power he had over the workers. Instead I saw that he had no authority or respect, how degrading his job was, and just how barbaric was the sugar estate where we lived. I saw that the sugar industry was serviced by brute labour that was managed with the utmost cruelty; no one escaped, neither master nor slave. The master watched the slaves like vultures and swooped down to gnaw at their humanity if they faltered in their labour. The culture of surveillance and division led to everyone always spying on each other. The white women used binoculars to watch the servants and workers, to see what they stole from their gardens, fruit trees and clotheslines, to see if they were having sex on their lawns, under their trees and in the ditches – which they did, frequently. People were always having sex out in the open; it was a common sight to see them at it, just like the animals that roamed free on the estate. I learned about sex from seeing the workers doing it in the canefields, in the canals and drains, under the bridges. Even the white overseers and their wives and lovers had sex out in the open. My mother and her servants were always gossiping and joking about who they saw having sex, and where. They took pleasure in discussing what they saw. I would notice how my mother's eyes lit up when they talked about sex. I saw that she liked sex and got excited just thinking about it. There, in our kitchen, in a huddle with the black and Indian women servants, I saw how sexual she was. I also saw it in how she behaved with my father. I knew when they were having sex, I knew the noises they made, and that they liked to do it in unlikely places at unlikely times – after midnight in the dark on the veranda or under a tree in the middle of the lawn. If the overseers had their binoculars trained on our house, as they often did, they were bound to see them.

The sugar estate gave me the feeling that very little divided beast and man. Both laboured, copulated, procreated and died exposed to the elements: in the mud, rain and canals, at the mercy of alligators, snakes, rats, vultures, mosquitoes and flies that sucked their blood and ate their flesh. The worst possible living conditions existed on the estate. I don't know how we did not all die of disease. The workers used open cesspit latrines in their living quarters, and at work in the fields, they shat and urinated on the land. You could see faeces floating in the canals and ditches where children played and people copulated. They even drank the same water they shat in. My father worked in the fields where he policed the workers, and daily witnessed these bestial conditions. He, personally, inflicted these working conditions. It is no wonder his own behaviour was so degenerate. He was always full of self-disgust. He hated himself because he hated what he was. They called him *Fulaman coolie overseer*. The Hindu workers hated him for being an Indian like them, who oppressed them. I think he was reduced by what he witnessed and endured daily on the estate. So while the high salary he earned there helped him buy a better standard of living, it also reduced him to self-disgust and self-loathing. In Berbice, he began to despise himself more than he did when we were poor on the East Coast and had no money. The richer my father became, the more ill and pitiful he grew. I think it made him insane. My mother and my sisters never noticed. They were too busy enjoying his new wealth, and the white man's lifestyle. I felt sorry for him. The suffering inside him showed.

The white overseers wore regulation khaki clothing and huge British walking boots, like a military uniform. They were made for big white men working in the colonies. They never fitted my father but swallowed him, so he looked comical, like an Indian Charlie Chaplin.

The factory was the only part of the estate where you found human genius and creativity. I loved the technology, especially the instrumentation for the centrifuges. When I told my father I wanted to become an engineer and improve their design, he said that was good because I would not have to work with people, only machines.

My father had no social life. He did not share the culture of the overseers who went to the social club to relax by reading foreign newspapers and magazines, drink at the bar, and play darts and snooker. There were parties at the club to celebrate birthdays and wedding anniversaries, promotions and retirements. For the non-whites like us to be invited was just an occasion to test if we were capable of mixing with them, whether our dress and speech were acceptable, or our table manners. Everything about us was tested on these occasions. To test and put us in our place was the only reason to invite us.

On Sundays, the white overseers took their wives and children to the club to spend the entire day there lunching, swimming, having tea, and playing sports.

Imran told me the Carreras were always there on

Sundays, and he often played snooker with Mr. Carrera while his wife looked on.

On the first Sunday I went to the club with Imran, the Carreras were eating lunch – steak and potatoes with peas. I decided to order the same and sit and eat with them. Imran liked whisky so I told him we should have a whisky each, and drink it while we waited for our meal to arrive. We had pre-planned how we would do this one Sunday. Most of the white overseers drank whisky. I saw there was a certain confident masculinity involved in being able to step up naturally to the bar, greet the bartender by his first name and ask for scotch-on-the-rocks. I did not do it myself, I left it to Imran, and he carried it off. In addition to the Carreras, there were three other families there. I could feel their eyes on us, two Coolies trying to act like white men. I knew we could easily be thrown out, but we might also be accepted. The overseers used the Hindu waiters as bouncers, and I half expected one of them to throw us out.

With my stomach full of whisky and my blood heating up, I felt man enough to stand near the snooker table and watch a Scottish overseer, McNeice, play with his two sons, Peter and Tony, whom I usually avoided if I ran into them on the estate. They were obviously uncomfortable with me watching them, and kept giving me resentful looks.

When our meal arrived, we took our trays to the dining table. I sat directly opposite Anne Carrera so I could observe her. Her proximity thrilled me but her husband's made me nervous. He sat so close to her, their arms touched.

As I sat there opposite her, I found myself trying to ascertain whether she was Chinese, and I found myself remembering the Yhips in Enmore, where I grew up.

★　　★　　★　　★

To grow up on a sugar estate in British Guiana when I did, at the height of British colonialism, before Cheddi Jagan began to try to liberate the estate workers, you grew up used to a horrible daily spectacle of Indian misery and poverty that made you nervous and anxious. I was always seeing Indian people like me, coolies, beggars, with flat bellies and skeletons that protruded from under their skin, walking with their hands outstretched, palms upturned and cupped. In Enmore, starvation was so bad that when a farmer came in with a sack of rice on a donkey cart, people engulfed him and emptied the sack in seconds. The same happened when the baker rode in on his bicycle with a basket full of bread or when a fisherman brought in a catch. All this hunger gave me nightmares about dying of starvation, and a desperation to escape poverty.

There was only ever one thing that gave me relief from my fear and terror of East Indian poverty – the Yhips' shop, or as people called it, the "Chinee shop".

The shop was just a small cottage, as humble as the workers' cottages, made of the same materials – a zinc roof over a simple wooden structure clad in wooden shingles. It was divided into sections – the cake shop at the front and, at the rear, the kitchen, sitting room and bedroom where the Yhip family lived. Anyone could come into the shop at any time by climbing the wooden ramp, and entering the open space around which ran a bench. Across the centre ran the counter where Mr. Yhip always sat, waiting to take your order and serve you. On the counter were glass cases full of the cakes and snacks made by his wife – Chinese and creole cakes she baked in clay ovens in the garden every Friday. She also made drinks that Mr. Yhip bottled every morning and placed in the rusting kerosene refrigerator he was always repairing.

The Yhips lived and worked in the cottage, so when you entered the shop, you were entering their home like a guest. Like guests, the customers sat on the benches, put up their feet and settled for a long visit, taking as long as possible to consume their cakes and drinks.

Factory workers and canecutters on their way to and from work liked to stop in for snacks Mrs. Yhip prepared specially for them. I often watched her make them fish-cake sandwiches. She would carefully slice open a large loaf of bread, butter it, insert a fish cake, place it in the middle of the loaf with pepper sauce, then go to her garden and return with a handful of lettuce, shallot and tomato to embellish the sandwich, then she wrapped it in a sheet of brown paper and labelled it with the name of the customer. She did all this with great care, almost lovingly.

There were usually more spectators than paying customers in the Yhip shop – children, beggars, cripples, the frail and elderly – who would sit there gazing hungrily and longingly at the food on display in the cabinets. It was not unusual for the Yhips to occasionally hand out food for free to the most hungry spectators, especially the old and infirm women. Along the shelves were glass jars full of sweets of different colours and shapes made by Mrs. Yhip that attracted the children. I was one of those children. When I had money, I always went to the shop, and stayed there a long time, simply sitting and watching the Yhips at work, salivating over the snacks on display and the delicious chilled home-made drinks in the refrigerator.

I never saw the Yhips receive thanks or praise for their hospitality. People on the estate were not accustomed to human decency and acts of kindness. They were used to racial abuse and cruelty and this is what they gave the Yhips in return for their hospitality and generosity. I was touched by the patience of the Yhips in putting up with so much abuse and persisting day-in-day-out with running their shop with such good grace under such hostile conditions. Nothing touched or moved me like seeing the Yhips at work in their shop, always filled with the smell of cakes baking in the ovens, and the Chinese food they made in their kitchen. In my childhood, those scents had a sedative effect on me. They always have done, and still do. The effect of Chinese people and their food and culture was always to give me a sense of peace – it was the best medicine for me. I liked to go to the shop just to watch how kindly the couple behaved and their dignity in the face of insults thrown at them. There was a beggar called Harold in Enmore village, whom the children stoned and chased. His legs were covered in purple sores. He always sat outside the Yhip shop. Sometimes Mrs. Yhip sent him to the back of the shop to sit in her garden. There she would pour water and disinfectant over his legs, dry them, give him clean clothing to wear and give him a plate of hot food. Mr. Yhip gave him a razor to shave his face. When he reappeared you could see that Harold was really a young and handsome man. In time, Harold became healed of his sores, like a miracle, and I became convinced that Mrs. Yhip possessed the gift of miracle which was her kindness, and this had healed and transformed Harold and brought him back to life. If an impoverished old woman asked for a cup of rice or some bread and butter, Mr. Yhip did not hesitate to give it. It was not only the delicious smells and sight of food we spectators went to the shop for, but also to see the gestures of kindness and mercy the Yhips performed. Growing up on a sugar estate, it was the only civilised behaviour I ever knew.

As I sat opposite Anne Carrera at the social club that Sunday at Rose Hall Estate in Berbice, I experienced something like the tranquillity I used to feel when I sat with the Yhips in their shop at Enmore Estate on the East Coast, Demerara.

Whether Anne Carrera was Chinese or not did not interest me, yet I could not help noting that Anne Carrera did not bear the slightest resemblance to the Yhips, who looked more like other Chinese people I had seen in Georgetown than they looked like Anne Carrera.

When I went to Georgetown to visit my cousins, I was used to seeing Chinese people working in their shops, or going about minding their business. It gave me a general impression of what Chinese people looked like. Anne Carrera looked nothing like these people and, remembering them, I understood the point my mother's servants made about the general physical characteristics of the Chinese, and Anne Carrera not having them, and looking more like a white woman. In my heart I was not interested in this gossip about their general physical characteristics, only their human ones. The Yhips and Anne Carrera had humanity in common in a country where I did not see much humanity. Their race did not interest me, only their kindness in a world full of unkindness.

Across the table from me, sitting near her very tall, big white husband, Anne Carrera did not look like a Chinese but a White, and she was eating like a White, like the English people at the club. She was using her knife and fork with the most ostentatious refinement, cutting her steak and chips into tiny pieces, collecting them painstakingly on the prongs of her fork along with a few green peas, as if threading them with a needle, before placing it all carefully in her mouth and chewing discreetly, showing nothing at all of the anxiety and nervousness of my family when they used knives and forks. Her husband and sons ate just like her. I felt uncivilised sitting opposite them, watching them eat in such a way while Imran and I were just shovelling large cuts of steak and chips into our big mouths, chewing like manatees until we washed and gulped it all down with swigs of Coca Cola.

Her husband looked big and strong and extrovert in his self-assurance, like all the white overseers. They liked to swagger and impress their authority on you, to let you know they were your master. He did not have a British accent, yet spoke what my mother called "good" English, that is the Standard English spoken by educated locals. The servants said he was a Portuguese passing himself off as white, and his wife was just copying him. I had no experience of a Portuguese community in which to place him. I only ever saw Portuguese people in passing when I used to visit Georgetown with my parents and they would point to people as if pointing to animals in a zoo, and say, "Them is Putagee people." To me, they looked exactly like white people, so when I looked at Mr. Carrera, who was allegedly Portuguese, I saw a white man. Therefore, I settled for thinking of the Carrera family as white, including Anne Carrera.

Not only did the overseers confine our lives, so did we. In Berbice, Muslims were a tiny part of the population. Only the rich ones stuck together, mainly to do business, mainly men. Otherwise, we met when we occasionally went to the mosque for prayers. On the East Coast and in Georgetown, we had a small community of extended family for our social life, mainly my mother's sisters and their children, but we lost touch with them when we moved to Berbice. For a time, we struggled to maintain contact, mainly through an exchange of visits among the cousins, but we were only children, hardly a community capable of giving me a strong sense of my Muslim identity. Even on the East Coast, we lived mostly among Hindu Indians and Black Christians. I went to a Church of England school where I started the day with Christian hymns and prayers. At Easter and Christmas, I had to go to church where I was not allowed to take communion, and had to learn more Christian hymns and prayers. It taught me I was not a Christian, and not a real Muslim, that I was a Muslim only historically, because my ancestors were supposed to have originated in a Muslim part of India: Kashmir.

Not until I went to South East Asia and the Middle East did I experience what it is like to be a real Muslim and have a strong sense of my Muslim identity. That, and 9/11, turned me into a Muslim, but it took a whole lifetime.

My cousin Sean had lived in London for many years but often returned to British Guiana. When I was conducting my campaign to penetrate the overseers' social club, I decided to invite him to Berbice, with the intention of taking him to the club and getting him to help me make an impression. He was just like an Englishman, fair-skinned, and fond of dressing to look like the Beatles. My parents called him a little white man, because he spoke just like one. He was so English, I could not see how the overseers might disapprove of him.

When I first took Sean to the club, he lived up to expectation. He was at ease there. He was used to English pubs. At the bar, he asked for a lager. I had no idea what that was. With the lager in his left hand, he would approach an overseer with outstretched right hand, smile wryly, shake his hand and greet him warmly, using his English accent. He told me it was not just the accent that was important when socialising with the English, but also the content of the conversation, which must be restricted to small talk, or else they became bored. He gave me many tips that helped me. He told me never to win when I played competitive games with them because they hated losing to wogs. Growing up in London had made Sean manly and confident. With him, I felt manly and confident too. However, my father warned me to be careful. He explained that if any of the Indian workers holidayed in England, on their return, they were fired, because their experience of seeing English people doing lowly jobs and sometimes of using English prostitutes made them insubordinate to the English overseers. My father did not think the overseers liked Sean.

There was a corner of the club fitted with comfortable chairs where the overseers relaxed and had long, private conversations. The white women liked to sit there. One night, Anne Carrera was sitting there with a few other overseers' wives. Sean and I joined them, and he began to make small talk with them. It was going so well, I became overconfident and sat closer to Anne Carrera and innocently laid my arm along the back of the sofa. When the manager came in, he saw us in this cosy situation with the women. He sent over the Hindu head waiter to tell us to leave. For a week nothing happened and Sean and I continued to visit the club to drink lager and play darts. Sometimes, Anne Carrera and her friends came in and waved to Sean, but they never got cosy on the sofa with him again.

On a Saturday night, Sean liked to have fun. He said that in London, he was used to spending Saturday nights at a pub or club, chatting up new women and picking one up for sex. He got me to drive him into town to the only night club there. He was in his element, drinking rum on the rocks, chatting up and dancing with women. It was late when a small group of overseers and their wives arrived, just before the dancing started. They played the racy calypsos. To my shock, Anne Carrera was the most enthusiastic dancer. She danced with abandon, winding her hips. Sean danced close to her, winding his hips and hugging her. In a matter of seconds, the overseers gathered their wives and left.

The next morning, Sunday, the manager's head servant, a Hindu, came to our house with an order for my father to present himself for a meeting. An overseer was only summoned to the manager's house to be reprimanded privately, of if there was an emergency. From his facial tic on his way out, I could tell my father was having an anxiety attack. When he returned, he ordered Sean to pack his bags and leave, then he gave me a thrashing with the electric cord. He did not have to explain anything. Everyone knew how the grapevine worked. It was obvious news had gotten back to the manager about Sean's lewd dancing with an overseer's wife. There were consequences that created one of the biggest scandals on the estate.

That week, word spread like wildfire that because of his wife's lewd dancing with Sean, Mr. Carrera was being fired and sent to work at Ogle Estate on the East Coast, and they had one week to pack and leave. From my window, I saw the servants come and go between the overseers' houses, whispering to each other. The white women stood on their verandas openly training their binoculars on the Carrera house.

Did I feel sorry for Anne Carrera? No. She deserved her punishment for dancing like a Black, without shame or modesty. The day the van came to move them, and Mr. Carrera drove his family away in the black Wolseley, I felt as if I might cry, but I stopped myself.

*   *   *   *

That was January, 1961 – the worst year in British Guiana, the year people began to emigrate to Canada, to escape the race riots and later the prospect of a Black government led by Forbes Burnham. By June, a Black family, the Hamiltons, had moved into the Carrera house. Mr. Hamilton was the new Chief Accountant in the manager's office.

There were big changes happening in the country. My father said that a Black man, Forbes Burnham, was leading his supporters to attack Indian people and turning the country upside down so he could become the next Prime Minister, and he was demanding to see Black people in top jobs, so the estate had to start hiring Black overseers and this is why they brought in the Hamiltons. That was one change. Another was that I had passed the entrance examination to Berbice High School and was starting there in September.

*   *   * *

On my first day at school, when I entered the classroom, I could not bear the gaze of the pupils as they looked me over. I was afraid of being treated like a *Fulaman*, afraid I would be isolated and bullied. As I have said, I came from a very ingrown, isolated Muslim family that was unsure of what it meant to be Muslim, that was ashamed of being Muslim. On the East Coast, when we dressed in white for Friday prayers and walked to the mosque, we huddled together like sheep, trying to blend into a white mass or shape in which, like clouds, we could not be individualised. Sometimes we ran like sheep, we were so afraid of being seen. But in front of a class of pupils of different races who were staring at me, in my fear and terror I could not hide. I became drawn to a Chinese girl in the second row. I cunningly chose to sit just three rows behind her, so I could keep her in my sights. Her name was Alice Wong. That day, I felt I was opening a door into a new life and shutting the door behind me on an old life. Alice was the first person I saw when I crossed that threshold, and she became the symbol of my future, a reason to live.

Three rows behind Alice, I could keep her in my sights and hear everything she said. Each day, I observed her closely, to imprint her indelibly in my memory, because I knew it was as easy to lose someone like her as it was hard to find her.

One day, I followed Alice home after school, to see where she lived. She took the country bus and got off at the workers' village on the sugar estate. I saw her walk into the shop where she lived with her family, a shop that looked like the Yhip shop at Enmore. There was even a well-planted vegetable and flower garden round the shop, just like Mrs. Yhip's.

We estate pupils had a school bus to take us to and from school. Most days Alice cycled, so I persuaded my parents to buy me a bicycle. The morning after I got the bicycle, I waited by the roadside for Alice to appear and I simply joined her and cycled all the way to school with her. After school, I cycled back with her all the way to her home, and when we got there, I parked my bicycle with hers, and walked into the shop as if I were a customer. Her father was sitting at the counter, just like Mr. Yhip. I returned his calm gaze and said politely, "Good afternoon." He nodded to me as if I were a customer entering his shop, not doing anything to discourage me.

I followed Alice to the sitting room and when she sat down, I sat in the chair opposite her. She went to the shop and brought us two glasses of chilled mauby and two Chinese cakes. I ate and drank contentedly, feeling triumphant at so easily gaining entrance to her home. I could not imagine my father taking it as calmly as Mr. Wong if a young man barefacedly walked into our home to visit his daughter. For certain, he would have turned him back, he would not have let her serve him any food or drink, and she would have received a beating for it, but the Wong home was as quiet and calm in the face of my invasion as the Yhips' used to be when their home was full of malingerers.

As long as the Wongs did not object, I continued to cycle Alice home every afternoon and spend time with her having a cold drink and cake. I always said "Good afternoon" to her father. I always sat in the same chair, opposite her, watching her and saying nothing, while her mother and brothers came and went. I always left when her mother began to prepare dinner.

My friendship with Alice became the most important thing in my life. I did not know what love was but I told myself I loved her, and concluded love was the warm feeling of security, comfort and satisfaction I felt in her home, in the presence of her family when the air was full of the scent of cakes baking in the oven, and Chinese food being cooked in the kitchen. To this day those smells are still like a drug that sedates me instantly.

In the Caribbean, the Chinese were the most tenacious of all the ethnic groups, in how they settled there in spite of the inhospitable conditions, and domiciled themselves stoically in a hostile society. They did not suffer the degradation of being enslaved and subjugated to regimes of brute labour. Their women were not raped and forced into relations of sexual miscegenation with Europeans. In any Caribbean country, you could travel to the most remote and inhospitable parts and find a solitary, isolated shop with a Chinese family working to supply food for several villages, and even though they were treated like outsiders and subjected to racial taunts and torments, they did not complain or give up. They kept aloof from the degradation around them, behaving as if it were some accident or bad luck that had brought them to those inhospitable places. I saw them like this in Guiana, Trinidad and Jamaica. Their dignity was like a miracle to me, a child from a Muslim family destroyed by the brutality the Chinese endured and overcame with stoicism. After I left the Caribbean, I saw such Chinese people in the cities of the First World, where for the isolated, rural village shop, they had exchanged the takeaway restaurant in the inner city. Their courage always touched me in the same way the Yhips' first did. I always wished my family possessed a little of their powers of endurance and stoicism.

I think my fall from the tree left me with a half-dead body and that afterwards I moved among the living like a ghost. I was sure Alice's family were not happy about me visiting her, yet I just imposed myself on them, sitting in their home every afternoon staring at Alice and not saying anything, knowing they were too nice to make me unwelcome. I was not brought up with any manners. I never asked politely for anything, I just took what I wanted and did what I liked. I was confident I could get away with it, but I didn't. In time, Alice wrote me a letter asking me not to visit her at home any more and I stopped, though I contrived not to register this at all, and for the next forty years or more, I behaved like a rejected lover instead of an unwelcome guest. It suited me to believe in our romance, and that it was only she who had rejected me, not her family, that her rejection was that of a lover, not a family or a race. Now I see why I preferred to see it that way. I think I felt I had a better chance of one day winning Alice over if the rejection came from her, but if it came from her race, it was insurmountable, because in British Guiana race was insurmountable.

I never did much talking with Alice. I just sat and looked at her and watched her family come and go, stubbornly enjoying the feeling of getting inside and being part of their world – in spite of knowing that outside the world was changing, and a new politics was demanding that we all proved we belonged to the nation.

After Alice rejected me, the world went mad. There were race riots when the thing I most feared happened, and Blacks and Indians began to kill each other in a political power struggle. It created tensions at school. I did not have friends there, only Alice. The East Indians stuck together but I avoided them because they were mainly Hindus and I knew they hated Muslims. The Chinese were not implicated in the racial politics of the country and this gave Alice a neutrality that made her popular. To be her friend was to be politically innocent, but that changed when a new teacher, a Black woman, Margaret Duke, came to our school and Alice fell under her spell. Margaret Duke was just returned from Europe with a masters in linguistics and literature. After only a year, she improved exam results in French and Spanish and her classes began to attract the brightest pupils. She became a threat to the headmaster, Mr. Lalljee, and her male colleagues who, to counteract her influence and attract students to their classes, began to popularise the sciences. This political division became racialised, with Black pupils siding with Margaret Duke, Indian pupils with Mr. Lalljee and his Indian male teachers. Having no power in the mainly male Indian staffroom, Margaret Duke cultivated her powerbase in the classroom where she groomed selected pupils for stardom, ascribing to them extraordinary intellectual gifts and, like a black Jean Brodie, calling them *la creme de la creme*. Alice was one of her favourites and I think that Margaret Duke, seeing my attachment to Alice, came between us.

Once, Margaret Duke told me she thought I was giving too much importance to science subjects, to the detriment of my grades in French.

I retorted, "I don't need French. I am going to be an engineer."

She came back with, "But you might be an engineer in a French-speaking country."

"Never!" I said at once, and everyone laughed, including Alice.

Margaret Duke had made me look like a fool and she continued to look for opportunities to turn me into a laughing stock again and again. I never forgave her for that.

Alice was not so neutral or innocent as to not notice

the hostility between Margaret Duke and me. She would refer to our conflict, trying to get me to be conciliatory with Margaret Duke, whom she admired. It made me see that if Alice ever had to make a political choice between supporting Indians or Blacks, she would support Blacks. Guyana was a country where you had to choose between the two.

In 1963, we finished high school and went our separate ways without ever resolving the conflict Margaret Duke had created between us. When I met Alice again in 2006, she remembered my clashes with Margaret Duke so well, it startled me.

2

I was supposed to get off the train at Balham, but I fell asleep and it took me on to Tooting Bec. By some miracle, I stirred, shook myself awake, exited the carriage and made my way out, following the signs. Then I was standing in the cold South London air at a busy intersection where red double-decker buses were waiting at red traffic lights and pedestrians were rushing along the pavements – obviously the rush hour, like any city rush hour, people going home with bags of food and shopping, all their worries etched on their downcast, bloodless faces. One first-world city is much like any other – concrete, faceless, overcrowded and inhuman. I hate them all.

She had said on the phone, "There'll be á minicab office. Take a cab, give them the address, and they'll bring you here. I use that cab company all the time, they know the address, don't worry."

I found a minicab office, a room like a cage. Huddled in it were five or six Indian men, probably Muslim by the look of them. Sean had told me that most minicab companies in London seemed to be owned and run by Muslims – mainly Pakistanis.

It irritated me how the controller at the window snapped, "Where you going?"

"Manville Road," I told him.

"Mandeville Road?"

I had to repeat the address four times before he understood. They always pretend not to understand English. It always happens when Indian men meet in an English-speaking country. They pretend to each other not to comprehend English. It is a way of flagging a tribe they wish to keep unspoken. If I'd wanted, I could have affected an Indian accent. It can be fun to play cat- and- mouse with them, keep them guessing, but I didn't bother. It's a game. I play it in Toronto, Calgary or New York. In England, it's even better to simply disappoint them and use my North American accent, the more US the better. It always has a devastating effect on them to see an Indian like them and hear he has become completely American. As a rule, they don't go to the US, because they don't have the appetite for success it takes to live in North America. Of course, now it's even harder for them to get into the US these days, with the "war on terror". So they are stuck with their colonial masters in England. They prefer to live under the boot of the English, but no matter how hard they try, the English will never accept them.

I got a driver who was even more stupid than the controller. He dived straight into asking me where I was from.

I snapped, "Canada!" and waved away further questions. "I'm late, hurry."

I didn't tip him but flung a five pound note through the window, so he had to scramble to catch it. Nor did I say *thank you*. In England, they are always saying *please* and *thank you* and *sorry* unnecessarily. It's manners for its own sake, a waste of time, like so much about England and the English.

I didn't like the look of the block of flats where she lived. Even in the darkness, you could tell the white paint was peeling all over the exterior and it was neglected.

There was no one in, though she said she'd be there. I rang the bell for a long time, hoping that wherever she was, she would hear and come and greet me, her long lost childhood sweetheart, lost for forty years. Such an important occasion, and she'd chosen to be absent. It was not a good sign, nor was it good I'd fallen asleep and missed my stop. The train might have gone on and taken me further away, to Morden, the end of the line, and I would have been lost. If she'd known, she would probably have felt as pissed off with me as I was feeling with her for not being there. She would probably think I couldn't be bothered to stay awake to find her after forty years. How was I to tell her the reason I could not stay awake was old age, my sick stomach and the diabetes that made me so tired, I was always falling asleep?

I kept ringing the bell, leaning on it. There was the ringing in my left ear, then in the right ear, as if in a dream; I heard her voice say my name, "Sonny."

I could still recognise her voice. I was so sure she was standing behind me, I did not need to turn around. I did not want to turn around, knowing I would not find a sixteen-year-old Alice, but an Alice sixty years old like me. So I took my time turning, afraid she would not like what she saw. When I looked in the mirror, I never liked what I saw: my sour, sagging face, my bald head, my belly sticking out a foot in front of me.

I recognised her by her posture and the fall of her hair where she stood in the half-shadow, half-light. She always held her shoulders a little stiffly and tilted her head back or to the right, to keep her hair out of her eyes. She still did it.

She explained she'd gone out to buy milk so she could offer me tea and coffee, and apologised for keeping me waiting, then opened the door and I followed her in.

I noticed her English accent and manners, the price she paid for living so long in England.

As in the old days when I used to visit her in Berbice, I sat directly opposite her so I could keep my eyes on her. There was an expression of long-suffering – like her father's – that she used to wear sometimes, and I saw it now, a sign that she was nervous and worried about meeting me.

Her first question was, "Has life been good to you?"

I decided not to be shy about my wealth but display it, so I said, "I can retire now, I don't have to work any more. I'm a millionaire several times over."

Being English now, and like them not wanting to

show she cared about money, she assumed a disinterested expression and gave a patronising English response, "Good for you."

"How about you?" I asked, hoping to get her to be similarly candid and direct about her finances, and it worked.

"I'm divorced," she said. "I just sold my house. I'm using the money to give me a little pension, and I bought this small flat because it's economic to run on my small state pension."

Clearly, she was struggling to make ends meet. I was very calm and cool as we sat there talking, as if no time had passed since we last saw each other, but I was calculating my chances of finally getting her. I was sure she was doing her own calculations, too. It was the most obvious thing for us to do. I thought we must both be curious about the prospect of a relationship between us, now we were both divorced and free, but we were both pretending we were not excited to meet again.

I did not like her English way of flagging up discretion and prevaricating. She had become a prevaricating English woman; I had become a plainspoken, blunt North American who liked to cut to the chase.

"Your flat is too small," I remarked. "You need something bigger."

She shrugged. "It's big enough for me."

"Not for me," I joked. "I'm a North American now. I'm used to everything being big. Big houses, big cars. I just bought myself the latest Cadillac, a nice, *big* one. In England, everything is too small – the helpings they give you in the restaurants, the clothes they sell you in the shops. I don't like it. How long have you been living here?"

"Almost forty years in my old house. It was bigger than this, with a beautiful, sunny garden. I am sorry I sold it. I miss it. I am sorry I had to sell it."

Sean told me that since her stroke, her daughter Sophie had wanted them to live near each other, and was arranging for them both to buy homes in the country. They'd bought this flat as a temporary stopover. I knew everything. I'd done my research; Sean had been my spy, telling me all about her life in England.

I reassured her, "I will buy you another house like your old house. Don't worry." It was almost a proposal; I intended it to be. To show her I was deadly serious, I told her to look for a big house to buy, I would pay for it. I knew her flat was almost sold.

She was taken aback, but kept cool and pretended to play along with me. She almost certainly knew I was staying at Sean's and he had told me everything about her plans, but she pretended not to know, though I had called her from Sean's, and she pretended to regard it as a joke. She confessed she was starting to find London too stressful and unhealthy after the stroke and was thinking of moving to the country for fresh air and relaxation. Perhaps Sussex.

I told her, "You want to go country? I will go country. How about Canada? I live in Calgary. It's a beautiful, very clean, big modern city with plenty of space. You would love it. I have a big penthouse there. You can live with me there, or we can get a house in the suburbs near a lake."

She said, "Canada is too cold for me. I was in Toronto for one winter and I thought the cold would kill me."

I reassured her again. "It's a dry cold in Canada, not damp like here, not dark in winter like here. In Canada, the sun shines bright in winter. You will like it. In Alberta, we get the warm Chinook winds from the beautiful Rockie mountains. You like the arts? We have an arts festival every year in Banff up there in the mountains. You will love it. When we go, I will rent us a big cottage "

"I don't want to leave England. I want to stay near my children. I just moved to Balham to be near my daughter. What makes you think I want to go to Canada?"

"I want you to come to Canada. All these years I never stopped thinking about you and dreaming about you. I prayed one day we would meet again, and have the relationship we never had."

"You don't know me and you are proposing to me and planning my future?"

"*Our* future, *together*. Of course I know you. You are the same person I knew in Berbice. Sean told me you hadn't changed at all. I thought many times of coming to London to look for you. My cousin told me when you came to live here in 1970. I told him to keep an eye on you, and let me know if you are all right. He told me about your divorce. As soon as he told me you were ill, I knew it was time for me to come and get you and take care of you."

She feigned sarcasm, "Thanks for making plans for my life."

I got sentimental. "I always was interested in you. Remember our drives in Berbice, how we used to hold hands?"

"I don't remember holding hands with you!"

"I remember. We were high school sweethearts. My father let me drive his green Mini. I used to take you for drives to the Corentyne."

"You can't think about marriage to me. You don't know me; I don't know you. We are strangers. I never knew you in Berbice, I was too young. I know you even less now."

"What do you want to know? Ask me anything. I will tell you everything."

"How is your health. Is your arm better? You had a broken arm."

"It's the same. Did I tell you about my childhood accident, how I fell from a tree and broke my joints?"

"You told me you had a bad accident. You gave me no details."

Alice had become a journalist in London. She liked to gather information and get to the truth, and from the start, her conversation could be probing.

Just as we finished talking, the doorbell rang. It was her daughter, Sophie. From the look she gave me and her coolness, I knew right away that Alice had told her about me and she was here to look me over and protect her mother. Sophie did not look at all like her mother. There was not a trace of Chinese in her appearance. She looked like a dark-haired white girl in her twenties. Actually, she reminded me of Anne Carrera and the more I watched Alice and Sophie together, it began to dawn on me that perhaps Mrs. Carrera was never Chinese at all, but a mixed race woman like Sophie: only half Chinese. I could see that Alice and Sophie were on very loving terms. They hugged and kissed when Sophie arrived and when she left. All the time she was there, Sophie stood protectively near her mother and placed an arm around her, as if shielding her from me.

Alice had changed. She looked less Chinese, a little like her daughter. Her skin complexion had lightened from living so long in a cold country. Just like Anne Carrera, she could pass for white now. They were both very English, two Englishwomen keeping me at a safe distance. Sophie could not hide her distrust and suspicion. Everything she said to me ended with a question mark, to show she was sceptical about me. They talked about her son, Paul, in such a way as excluded me from knowing what they were talking about. They were showing me they were a close family, but I took it as snobbery and exclusion, especially from Sophie.

It reminded me of Anne Carrera and her two precious

sons, so long ago in 1961, so close and so loving there was no hope of me ever sharing what they had. It reminded me that though I admired and wanted what they had, I also resented it because I knew it would never be mine. I could never be part of it, never be one of them, because I was a *coolie*. Though I was a millionaire, I was still the coolie looking in from the outside on the lives of white people.

I returned to Calgary. Then for the next three months, I made my plans and phoned and emailed her every day. I proposed to her over and over and I laid out plans for our future in the Middle East. Then, because she was afraid of living there, I promised to buy houses for us anywhere in the world she wanted to live. She was dreaming of living in Barbados, so I promised her a house there. I promised to take care of her for the rest of her life. She wanted to know everything about my past, what I had done, year by year. For three months, I spilled out everything to her in emails and phone calls and yet at the end of it, she was still saying it was wrong that I wanted to marry her after forty years, when we didn't know each other at all.

From the start, I told her I wanted her to leave England; it was not a place I could live in, because I hate the English too much. She told me she loved England, so I questioned her why. She said it was because her friends and family were there and she loved them too much to leave them, especially her son and daughter. I told her that from now, we would be each other's friends and family, she wouldn't need anyone but me. I told her we would live in the Middle East, which I regard as my true home. Her response was typically English, based on thinking England and the English were better than anywhere or anyone else. She was worried about living in the Middle East because of restrictions on dress and freedom for women. I promised her we would live in Bahrain or Dubai where it is liberal and there are expatriate compounds where western women dress how they like and drink and smoke and swim in bikinis. I promised her that wherever we lived in the Middle East, she would have a house full of servants, chauffeur-driven cars and all the money she needed for the rest of her life.

"What kind of servants?" she asked me. "Filipino women? I hear they abuse them in the Middle East. They might think I am a Filipino and abuse me. I wouldn't feel safe there."

I reassured her. "You don't look like a Filipino woman, you are Chinese. No one will take you for a Filipino if you are with me. I will look after you. In Saudi Arabia, I am a V.I.P. I have contacts in the Saudi royal family. I have personal bodyguards."

Over and over she protested that I didn't know her, and it was wrong to ask her to marry me, that I was being rash in making plans for our future when we were strangers.

She was getting so angry and impatient with me on the phone and in her emails, I decided I had to return to

London and spend time with her, so she could satisfy herself we were not strangers. She had sold her flat and had to move soon, to follow Sophie who was already preparing to move with her fiancé. So, in July, I turned up at her flat in South London again, to help her move and test our relationship and see if we had a future together.

I am never comfortable in England. It takes me back too much to the estate in Berbice and the overseers who ran it. England was a country we did not know. The overseers made sure the culture would always be alien to us – the pubs, the newspapers, the clothing, the language, the jokes and references, the food. When we tried to socialise with them, the overseers would refer to all these aspects of English culture to alienate us, knowing it was unfamiliar to us, knowing it would make us feel left out and uncomfortable. They used England and Englishness to make us outsiders. Now the whole place made me as nervous as living on the estate used to make me, but Alice was comfortable in England, happy with being a journalist there, and with her friends and family near. It was going to be hard to get her out of there, but I had to be decisive. There was no longer any time to waste. I had already wasted too much time, so I thought through my plans carefully and returned to London to finally get her. I did not stay at Sean's this time, I stayed with her. She did not have a room for me so I bought a sofa for her living room and slept on it.

★   ★   ★   ★

We drove to Sussex a dozen times to look for a house. We found one with a sunny garden she loved, where she thought she could recreate a home like the one she'd had to sell, where she could plant a garden again. I persuaded her to contact her solicitor and instruct him to put in an offer. In addition to the money she would get for the flat, she needed eighty thousand pounds more, so I told her lawyer I was her fiancé and would provide it. He was a Guyanese Hindu. I think he only had to hear my Muslim name to decide not to trust me. He gave the usual spiel about money-laundering regulations, and demanded to see my bank statements and proof of identity: everything, my birth certificate, passports and utility bills, even though I told him we were getting engaged, and would be married by the end of the year. It was outrageous how he treated me like a criminal. I told her to dismiss him, but she always liked Hindus, as much as she liked Blacks. She said he was like a friend; he had helped her a lot with her divorce. I told her he was not helping her by treating me with so much hostility. She did not dismiss him, and then he added insult to injury by advising her to make a prenuptial agreement to protect her property. It caused a big quarrel between us. I told her that if we were going to marry, I would expect more loyalty from her. Every day, she talked to her friends and family, and confided everything to them. I used to overhear their telephone conversations. She was telling them every single thing about me. She made no decision unless she sounded out her son, daughter and close friends.

It meant I had to meet these people and gain their approval and acceptance. She was not going to marry me unless they approved. It took me back to the culture of surveillance on the sugar estate, where we had to pass through unwritten tests set by the overseers before we were allowed to live with them. Before I even began to meet her family and friends, I rejected their influence over her. I told her I was not interested in marrying them, only her. It upset her but I had to have things on my terms. I had struggled to get to a position where I would not to let anyone stand in judgement of me any more. I was not a *coolie* any more.

I would tell her often how seeing my son with his wife, a Chinese girl, Kin, who was his high-school sweetheart whom he'd married, made me remember how we'd been high school sweethearts, and how it had made me think I should have married her.

The first time I mentioned Kin on that second visit, she gave me a look of deadly seriousness, and asked, "Are you jealous of your son?"

It was one of the many Freudian questions she was to bombard me with, that she herself would then answer. She told me, "I noticed in your emails, you talk a lot about your daughter-in-law, Kin, and her son. You like to give them both a lot of money, and look after them. You do the same with your daughter, Fatima. Don't you think your son, Neal, should provide for his wife and son, not you, and shouldn't your daughter's husband be looking after her, not you? Aren't you undermining your son and your son-in-law with your money?"

It was obvious she had absorbed every bit of information about my life she had extracted from me in our phone calls and emails over the last three months, turned it all over, inside out, and formed a negative picture of me. She was always saying I used money to control my family.

I tried to joke it away. "O.K., Mrs. Freud, I surrender. You know me better than I know me." But if I threw her off one scent, she would quickly pick up another.

She wanted to know the cause of my divorce, which I kept refusing to discuss.

Finally, I told her. "After I left Berbice, I got a job as an electrical engineer on Enmore Estate, where I grew up. I lived in Georgetown. I used to drink too much, and would speed on my motorcycles. I had accidents, once on my own, once with my ex-wife, Amina, before we were married, and we ended up in Georgetown Hospital in beds next to each other, both of us in plaster. Her family were very very angry. They used to come to the hospital and fight with me and my parents every day. They threatened to sue me and my parents for financial compensation and make us bankrupt. I was very scared; so were my parents. In the end, they told me I had to marry her and we agreed. They arranged the marriage in just a week. One day we were in hospital in plaster, the next, getting married, covered in bruises, our injuries showing. I married her for the wrong reasons, because I felt guilty about the accident, and to stop my family going bankrupt. The marriage was a disaster. She was promiscuous. She was always looking at other men. The women in her family were like that, oversexed. Her two aunts offered me sex but she doesn't know it. If she did, it would have destroyed her.

I felt so sad when I was telling Alice how I came to be married. She had no idea how much pain it caused me, that marriage, and it was because it was so painful that I'd dreamed of her all the time.

I've always felt, had I married Alice, I would never have been forced into marriage with Amina. Alice would have saved me from that. I think one of the reasons I wanted to marry her in 2006 was to give myself the feeling I could go back in time, change my life and forget my tragic marriage.

The more I told Alice, the more ammunition it gave her to analyse me and probe me further.

She asked me several times, "You are always talking about your ability to destroy women, especially your ex-wife and your mother. Why?"

I told her, "There are secrets in my family that are dangerous. You have secrets. I never knew you liked my brother, Rupert."

She said, "Everyone liked Rupert. He was warm and affectionate."

I decided to tell her about Rupert and Amina.

"My wife liked him too. In 1976, he wanted to come to Canada, so I helped get him there, and he came to Toronto live with me, my wife, my son and daughter. It was a mistake. He slept with my wife; I caught them in bed. That is what ended my marriage, but nobody knows; it's a secret. If her parents and our children found out, it would destroy her because they would have nothing to do with her; no one would respect her. She would be isolated, finished."

"Is that what you would like to happen to her? Do you think she should be punished?"

"If I'd wanted to punish her, I wouldn't have bought her a penthouse, a sports car, and be setting up a massive pension fund for her."

"Yes you would. You are making her dependent on you and grateful to you."

"Why would I want to do that? I don't love her. I love you."

"That's the best reason for doing it. You are denying her love by giving her money. You know very well money does not bring happiness; you are not giving her happiness. You only have to stop her money, and she is finished. That is how you will destroy her. Maybe you are angry you were forced into marriage with her, and you want to punish her, 'destroy' her as you say."

She asked me, "Where does your mother come into

this secret? Why do you say you can destroy your mother too?"

"Because of Rupert. She will know it's her fault Rupert did what he did to me and destroyed my life."

"How will she know?"

I told her my final, biggest secret. "Rupert is not really my brother. His father is not my father. My mother had him by another man, a Hindu overseer at Enmore named Sukdeo. The day I went up the genip tree in 1957, Sukdeo was with my mother in our house. I was trying to see what they were doing in the house. I saw them having sex. That is why I fell.

So, Alice got all my secrets out of me. I could not believe how Alice could be doubting my integrity when I was giving her eighty thousand pounds to buy herself a house in Sussex. With the proceeds of the sale of her flat, and eighty thousand pounds, she could get the house she wanted. It was all going through, the legal paperwork and so on. I had decided to sell my CNRL shares to raise the cash so I could marry Alice and start our life together.

When I offered to provide eighty thousand pounds cash to buy the house in Sussex, I was absolutely confident the sale of my CNRL stocks would provide that amount. I got her to instruct her solicitor, the Hindu, to proceed with making the offer for the house and reassured him I would provide the cash in time. Unfortunately, the sale price of the stocks dropped and I could not provide the cash in time. It was a disaster. It made her family and friends suspicious of all my financial promises, especially her son who asked me to meet him to discuss my offer to buy his mother a house. He said he was discussing things with his mother and certain things worried him. I reassured him I was doing it because I loved her and wanted to look after her. I did not want the house; she could keep it in her name. He said he was still suspicious of my offer and overstepped the mark by telling me it was not necessary for me to give his mother money, she was capable of buying herself her own home. He even suggested I might be playing a strange game of revenge whereby I would lull Alice into a false sense of security, letting her think she was financially secure with me, then I would cruelly take it all away by suddenly ending our marriage. I asked him how it was possible that giving his mother eighty thousand pounds could be revenge, and he suggested that it was because she had "dumped" me when we were young and I wanted to get her into a position where I could dump her back.

From my conversation with him, he struck me as being a typical young Englishman, not used to living in a country where you grow up feeling confident you can acquire wealth easily. He did not grow up respecting people like me who made money, but distrusted them. This is England and the English for you. Because of my offer to provide Alice with financial security for the rest of her life, it made her English family and friends suspicious of me.

As if it were not bad enough she had become so English, it turned out Alice had married a Jew, and her name was so Jewish. I told her it would be impossible for her to move about the Middle East freely with me with such a name. She would be taken for an Israeli spy, and I could not afford that, because my job was highly classified and her children with their Jewish name could not come and visit her in the Middle East.

Not only did she interrogate me about my money, she continued to probe my private life. She kept returning to the theme of why my marriage ended, why I said it would destroy my family if the reason got out.

I was offering to make her a rich woman if she married me, but it was not enough. She distrusted me, perhaps because she distrusted Muslims now and sided with Jews, as she used to side with Blacks.

My job is sensitive, so I had to test Alice's politics. I started from the day after I arrived, a Friday. I told her it was Friday and I needed to find the nearest mosque, to pray. I asked her, "Where's the nearest mosque?"

I thought she had always known I was not a practising Muslim, and was not going to take me seriously, but she did. To my surprise, she got out the Yellow Pages to look for a mosque. All these years, I thought she knew I was not a practising Muslim, only one in name. I laughed and told her I was only joking about going to a mosque. She was embarrassed, and said she knew that to Sean being a Muslim was important.

I acted innocent. "Oh yes? I didn't know it was important to Sean."

"He told me he sometimes goes to prayers at your cousins'."

I said dismissively, "My family are not real Muslims. We are like those Christians who only go to church at Christmas. Going to a mosque to pray does not make you Muslim."

"Were you brought up Muslim?"

"You mean a *fulaman*? Of course not. I did not like being a Muslim in the Caribbean. They hate us. I wanted to be Chinese like you. I idealised you. I went looking for you in every Chinese woman I met and in every South East Asian country I went to. I've been all over the world looking for you. I never found anyone like you, but I found myself in the Middle East, the true home of real Muslims. I want it to be my home now. I'd like you to live there with me."

I think it was hearing how seriously I took my Muslim identity and that I had a top-secret job that made her decide to introduce me to her friend, Romesh. That, and the time I had spent showing her documentaries about 9/11 on my laptop, showing her that the twin towers and Pentagon were never actually blown up and that there were no Muslim terrorists who ever flew planes into them. I told her Muslim terrorism did not exist. I also showed her my research on the Illuminati to try and show her that the Jews are a mafia and they blew up the World Trade Center.

I think my pro-Islamic, anti-Israel, anti-Blair, anti-Bush politics worried her, and that is why she needed to bring in her political friend, Romesh, to check me out.

I hired a car and we drove to Middlesex to meet Romesh, who I began to realise was her best friend. I was uneasy and nervous about meeting him because she acted as if his opinion of me was going to be the most important of anyone's. The night before, there'd been a documentary on the television and he'd appeared in it, in his role as a civil rights lawyer. The way she spoke about him, it was obvious he meant a lot to her. Whether it was a personal or professional relationship, I was uncertain and she kept me guessing.

I noticed CCTV cameras outside his house. I had gone and hired a car and a cell phone. It was making me nervous. In England, there are surveillance cameras everywhere that register car licence plates and in England they keep cell-phone data and store it for two years. I was leaving my footprints all over England.

From the start, I did not like Romesh, and he did not hide his distrust of me. As soon as I met him, I knew he'd made the most obvious assumptions about me, and I could tell Alice had already discussed me with him in detail because only she could have given him the information about me that he had. For example, he wanted to know whether I'd flown in from the Middle East and encountered any difficulties with security.

I asked innocently, "Why should I have difficulties?"

He said disarmingly, "Well, it's the times in which we live, isn't it? With the so-called war on terror, and you have a Muslim name."

"And I look Muslim, right?"

"Yes, you do."

I asked him innocently, "And would you have trouble with security when you travel?"

"If you are Asian, they think you are an illegal immigrant, so they do check me carefully."

"But you travel with a European or British passport, right?"

"Right."

"And what are you? British or Indian?"

"I'm British. I grew up here. I came here from Kenya."

"Yes, I notice you guys are very well integrated here. You all sound so English, you are like Englishmen. You Hindu guys are good at being English."

In the best US accent I could do, I told him I was a North American and proud of it. I knew it would annoy him because Alice told me he was a Marxist who hated America, another Hindu revolutionary like Cheddi Jagan, who destroyed Guyana.

I treated him like an Englishman, like an English overseer, because he had their accent and their patronising, superior ways of making you feel like an outsider. I also saw he was trying to show Alice he did not trust me. He asked me too many questions and he talked like a chameleon, always changing faces and switching from innocence to cunning.

I told him that when I travelled, I was searched for box cutters.

He asked, "Really? At which airports do they do that?"

I told him, "The white countries – Italy, France, Germany, Australia, South Africa, New Zealand."

He flattered me. "Wow! You travel a lot! Do you go to those places on holiday?"

I told him I travelled on business, and was going to Holland soon.

He wanted to know what kind of business I ran.

I told him. I explained my business was designing the instrumentation for centrifuges. That I had started off in the Caribbean with sugar ones, then in Canada, South East Asia and Canada, I'd moved into gas centrifuges when I started work in the oil sands of Alberta, where I work on the technology that separates sand from oil. I told him I had moved on to more modern kinds of centrifuges.

His conversation was like a game of chess. I knew he was waiting to checkmate me. He asked me where in Holland I was going. I told him I was going to Almelo. I saw a glint in his eye, so I asked him if he had heard about Urenco.

"Of course," he said. "They make the most complex, highly engineered machines in the world. You must be one of the best to work there."

I did not try to deny it; it was obvious he was on my trail, like Alice who was on my trail too, the trail of my private life, probing all my private secrets, while he probed my professional life. They were working as a team. I had walked into a trap.

I said simply, "Of course, I am."

I was tired of his cat-and-mouse conversation and decided to assume his interest was not in me but in Alice's well being. I behaved as if I were trying to impress him. I told him I was a highly paid international engineer who commanded the highest consultation fees, and so I could take care of Alice, but I could tell he was politically excited, and wanted to confide his suspicions to Alice. He asked her to join him in the garden and they sat out there talking for a long time. I am sure he was checkmating me, telling her why she must not trust me. I had overplayed my hand but Alice was demanding honesty from me and it was my way of being honest – leaving a trail she and Romesh, with their experience in political journalism, were capable of following. I thought with all I was offering her, nothing else would matter.

Meeting her best friend, Romesh the Hindu, made me even more certain I had to get Alice out of England. She had lived there almost forty years and had nothing to show for it, and was struggling to make ends meet on her meagre pension. The Guyanese Indians who went to Canada call it "the land of milk and honey" because it made them rich, and money had freed them. This did not happen to the Guyanese in England. In Canada I got my training in centrifuge instrumentation, and got sent to Saudi Arabia where I made my first million and was able to return to Canada and buy property that was now giving me massive profits. That was never going to endear me to the English in 2006.

In England, they pretend not to like money. Alice's friends and family were like that. When they heard I was giving her eighty thousand pounds to buy a house I did not want to own, they became hostile to me. This is so typical of the English, to assume they are superior to you when they are not. They behaved like that in their colonies, and now they have no power, they are still doing it. They told her not to trust me. One by one, they came to the flat to meet me, and I could tell that, like Romesh, they were all against me. I could tell this from the way she became more distant every time one of them met me. I knew she was going to reject me again as she had done in 1963, when she wrote me a letter in red ink, like blood, telling me not to visit her or try to see her again. In one of our phone calls after March, I asked her why she wrote me that letter. It had broken my heart so much. I wish she had let me go on believing she wrote me that letter like a lover calling off a relationship, but she told me her parents had made her write it. It devastated me. I could not bear to think her people did not want me; I thought it would be so easy to become one of them. I wanted that more than anything else. It's why I loved Alice so much, for almost forty years. When I went to London in 2006 to get her back, I wanted to repair the hurt and damage that their rejection had done to me. I thought I would do it, but by August, 2006 I knew she was going to reject me again, and I could not bear it. I thought it would foretell another disaster in my life, as it did the first time she rejected me, so I simply left the country without saying goodbye, accepting this time I would never see her again, not in this life, but perhaps in the next, which might be more free from disaster than this life has been for me.

3

I lived in times that became more not less dangerous for me.

When I lived in Guyana, no one knew anything about Muslims. Now, because of 9/11, the whole world knows about us. No one used to notice me. Now, I am finally seen for who I am. When the airport staff see me, their eyes flicker with recognition. They know I am a Muslim because of my Semitic face with my hawk nose and pointed beard, and it makes them afraid. Now I see the look of recognition I get when the security staff see me. Their eyes flicker like the lens of a camera. The war on terror freed me from my invisibility as a Muslim.

On 11 September, 2001, I was in my apartment in Calgary watching television when I saw United Airlines Flight 11 hit the North Tower. I jumped with excitement and anticipation because I knew there were many people in the building and they would begin jumping from the windows. Like the whole world, I watched and waited to see it and sure enough, soon they began to fall from a great height, just like I did in 1957 in British Guiana, when I fell from a tree. When people began to fall from those windows, I saw them spread open their arms and legs just like I did when I fell. Watching them fall, I relived my fall in 1957. I was aware millions of people were watching them fall and it made me feel that the whole world was finally seeing me fall too. It brought a strange relief, as if a lifelong, weighty burden of loneliness fell from me. You see, we all need to be seen for who we are. Watching them, I wondered why, when I fell, did I open my arms and legs like wings. Did I hope that I might fly? I think I did. I don't know what it was in me that made me think I might fly, maybe the same thing that made me fall in love with Alice Wong. Something in me needs to defy my limitations. It made me think I might be able to fly and save my life. In the same way, I thought that after almost forty years, I could turn back time and be young again with Alice Wong and make her love me. In 2006, just before I left her in England, she told me it takes a long time to learn what love is and she thought I did not know what it is. I agree with her. I've never known what it is, I still don't and I never will. She was my only reason for looking for love. I hoped we would find it together but it was not to be.

A few months after my return to Calgary, Sean sent me a copy of a documentary Alice was involved in making for British television. It was called "Nuclear Walmart". It showed me Alice had seen me for who I was all right – not the international oil engineer I told her I was. I told her I had worked with A.Q. Khan at Urenco, that I hoped to work in Iran etc. No doubt, with the help of her friend, Romesh, she put two and two together. I gave them enough leads. While she was researching it, she sent me emails with questions about the Pakistan nuclear procurement network. I was part of the network and I had helped develop the centrifuge technology in Almelo in Holland. In the Iranian war with Iraq, I developed designs and specifications for a complete plant of nuclear centrifuges. I was paid five million dollars for this. I was planning to live in the Middle East to be part of the Middle East nuclear procurement network because I believe Israel must be destroyed and Muslims must be free from the tyranny under which they have been placed. As an Arab Muslim, which I am now, I would never be called a *Fulaman*, never again.

After meeting Alice again in 2006, I returned to my Calgary apartment and waited for the right time to leave for the Middle East to live there for the rest of my life, to die there a Muslim in the Muslim world.

I did nothing but exist for the next few years, exist and watch the world go by. Outside, I saw the seasons change. On the television, I watched the politics of the war on terror change and how the fear of we Muslims continued to develop. I had hoped to take Alice to Dubai with me, but once I knew she'd found me out, I finally accepted she would never ever be mine and it was all over. Letting go of her began to change me for the better. I lost my ego and began to see myself as just a human being suffering from high blood pressure, high cholesterol and diabetes. When I returned to Calgary, knowing I was going to be alone for the rest of my life, I began to take care of myself. I became a health freak. I started to take vitamin supplements and, as they say, "listen to my body" and take care of it because I wanted to live and be healthy. She only ever wrote me once after we parted in 2006. She told me she did not love me, and never would because we were totally incompatible. She said I was only interested in giving her money and it was not enough; she needed warmth, affection, conversation and companionship from me and in the time we spent together, it was clear I could not give her these things. She said her Jewish husband used to give her those things and she was certain it was what she needed, not money. I laughed when I read that because I thought it was stupid for her to reject my money. Money is all you need to feel secure in this world. Yet, once I read that letter from Alice, and saw she did not want my money, I realised I had so much money I did not need her, and finally gave her up. I burned her letter, and enjoyed how the heat of the fire warmed my hands. It was cold and I loved that heat. It comforted me and I accepted she was gone forever. I was alone but I had myself. I was alive, I was rich, I could be warm and look after myself and I did not need her; she would never haunt me again. Before I went to look for her in London in 2006, I had had a minor heart attack that I survived. It terrified me and later I was diagnosed with diabetes, a disease that had plagued my family, leading to some of them having their limbs amputated, causing blindness and early death among others. It all filled me with fear and, looking back, I think it was my fear of suffering and dying alone that made me look for Alice in 2006.

When she rejected me in that letter, and I burned it, I decided I had to find a way of freeing myself from her. I could not continue to live my life possessed by a woman who did not want me. I had to learn to live alone, so I did that. I lived entirely alone, never seeing anyone, never thinking about her or remembering her. I suppressed my memory and lived only with myself, to prove to myself I did not need her. Then once I had repressed my memories of her, I let my memory be free to show me who I was and what to do. I would choose my destiny and calling as a true Muslim and return to the Middle East, to live as a Muslim and do the work of a Muslim, helping to build the nuclear programme that would lead to the destruction of Israel. Sometimes, in my Calgary apartment, I dressed in my thobe, tagiyah, ghutra and agal and admired how noble I looked, like a Muslim prince. But something unexpected happened. As a result of living alone for several years, with no one but myself for company, I got to know myself very well. I understood what my body wanted and how it behaved and I nursed it and came to enjoy my awareness of myself – my sleeping and eating patterns, my minor illnesses and making myself get better. I loved living alone and look-ing after myself without distractions. I began to feel very strong and healthy and well. One day, it dawned on me that I was perfectly happy and contented and I loved myself and I made the decision not to go to the Middle East but to continue to live by myself and enjoy my money and the rest of my life alone. I did not need a mission to justify my existence. I guess I have to thank Alice for this. If I had not gone to London to find her and she had not rejected me and sent me back to Calgary to live with myself, I might have blown up the world.

ABOUT THE AUTHOR

Jan Lowe Shinebourne (nee Lowe) was born in Guyana on Rose Hall Sugar Estate. She attended school on the estate, and then Berbice High School. She comes from the same area of Guyana as her near contemporaries, fellow writers Cyril Dabydeen and Arnold Itwaru. After she left school she went to work as a journalist in Georgetown. She attended the University of Guyana between 1968-1970. She began writing in the mid 1960s and in 1974 she was a prize-winner in the N.H.A.C Literary Competition.

In 1970 she moved to London where she still lives. She did postgraduate literary studies at the University of London. In addition to her work as an author, she has also worked in London as an editor for several journals, as a political and cultural activist and as a college and university lecturer. She has done reading tours in North America, Europe, the Caribbean and Asia, and was a Visiting Fellow at New York University.

She has published two novels , *Timepiece* (Peepal Tree Press, 1986) and *The Last English Plantation* (Peepal Tree Press, 1988).

ALSO BY JAN SHINEBOURNE

Timepiece
ISBN9780948833038; pp. 186; pub. 1986, reprinting; price:
£8.99

Sandra Yansen must leave behind the close ties of family and village when she goes away to take up a job as a reporter in Georgetown. But she feels that leaving Pheasant is a betrayal and is confused about where she stands in the quarrel between her mother Helen, who is pro-town and her father, Ben, who is deeply attached to the country and its values.

She finds the capital riven by racial conflict and the growing subversion of political freedom. Her newspaper has become the mouthpiece of the ruling party and she finds her ability to tell the truth as a reporter increasingly restricted. In the office she has to confront the chauvinism and vulnerability of her male colleagues whilst at the same time finding common cause with them in meeting the ambivalent challenges of Guyana's independence.

Yet, uncomfortable as she frequently is in the city, Sandra knows that she is growing in a way that Pheasant would not allow. But when Sandra is summoned home with the news that Helen is seriously ill, and re-encounters the enduring matriarchy of her mother's friends, Nurse, Miss K., Noor and Zena, she knows once again how much she is losing. It is their values that sustain Sandra in her search for an independence which does not betray Pheasant's communal strengths.

Fred D'Aguiar wrote of *Timepiece* 'recovering a valuable past for posterity and enriching our lives in the process' and Ann Jordan in *Spare Rib* reviewed it as 'not a novel to be taken at face value, for its joy lies in the fact that it works on so many different levels... the subtleties and tensions of life are not far from the surface as the author questions the notions of political as well as individual dependence and independence'. *Timepiece* won the 1987 Guyana prize.

The Last English Plantation

ISBN 9781900715331; pp. 182; pub. 1988, 2001; price: £8.99

'So you want to be a coolie woman?' This accusation thrown at twelve year old June Lehall by her mother signifies only one of the crises June faces during the two dramatic weeks this fast-paced novel describes. June has to confront her mixed Indian-Chinese background in a situation of heightened racial tensions, the loss of her former friends when she wins a scholarship to the local high school, the upheaval of the industrial struggle on the sugar estate where she lives, and the arrival of British troops as Guyana explodes into political turmoil.

Merle Collins writes: 'Jan Shinebourne captures the language of movement, mime, silences, glances, with a feeling that comes from being deep within the heart of the Guyanese community. In *The Last English Plantation* her achievement lies in having the voices of the New Dam villagers dominate the politically turbulent period of 1950s Guyana – A wonderful and stimulating voyage into the lives behind the headlines, into the past that continues creating the changing present. The voices of the New Dam villagers never leave you.'

Wilson Harris writes: 'Jan Shinebourne's *The Last English Plantation* is set within a labyrinth of political chaos in British Guiana in the 1950s. But the novel is more subtly as well as obsessively oriented towards the psychological as well as the inner landscape of a colonial age. A gallery of lives depicted in *The Last English Plantation* is drawn from diverse strata of cultural legacies and inheritance. The desolations, the comedy of adversity, the contrasting moods of individual and collective character give a ritual, however incongruous, substance to the fate of a dying Empire.'

The Godmother and Other Stories
ISBN: 9781900715874; pp. 160; pub. 2004; price: £7.99

Covering more than four decades in the lives of Guyanese at home or in Britain and Canada, these stories have an intensive and rewarding inner focus on a character at a point of crisis. Harold is celebrating the victory of the political party he supports whilst confronting a sense of his own powerlessness; Jacob has been sent back to Guyana from Britain after suffering a mental breakdown; Chuni, a worker at the university, is confused by the climate of revolutionary sloganizing which masks the true situation: the rise of a new middle class, elevated by their loyalty to the ruling party. This class, as the maid, Vera, recognises, are simply the old masters with new Black faces.

The stories in the second half of the collection echo the experience of many thousands who fled from the political repression, corruption and social collapse of the 70s and 80s. The awareness of the characters is shot through with Guyanese images, voices and unanswered questions. It is through these that their new experiences of Britain and North America are filtered. One character lies in a hospital in London fighting for her life, but hears the voices of her childhood in Guyana – her mother, African Miss K, the East Indian pandit and the English Anglican priest. Once again, they 'war for the role of guide in her life'. In 'The Godmother' and 'Hopscotch', childhood friends reunite in London. Two have stayed in Guyana, while one has settled in London. The warmth of shared memories and cold feelings of betrayal, difference and loss vie for dominance in their interactions.

These stories crystallize the shifts in Guyana's uncomfortable fortunes in the post-colonial period, and while they are exact and unsparing in their truth-telling, there are always layers of complexity that work through their realistic surfaces: a sensitivity to psychological undertones, the evocative power of memory and a poetic sense of the Guyanese physical space.

RECENT FICTION FROM PEEPAL TREE

Angela Barry
Goree
ISBN 9781845231255; pp210; July 2010, £9.99

Myriam Chancy
The Loneliness of Angels
ISBN 9781845231224; pp365; March 2010, £12.99

Kwame Dawes
Bivouac
ISBN 9781845231057; pp210; March 2010, £9.99

Brenda Flanagan
In Praise of Island Women & Other Stories
ISBN 9781845231279; pp144; October 2010, £8.99

Manzu Islam
Song of Our Swampland
ISBN 9781845231705; pp336; November 2010, £12.99

Diana McCauley
Dog-Heart
ISBN 9781845231231; pp242; March 2010, £9.99

All Peepal Tree titles are available from the website
www.peepaltreepress.com
with a money back guarantee, secure credit card
ordering
and fast delivery throughout the world at cost or
less.

E-mail: contact@peepaltreepress.com